ABOUT THE BOOK

It's hot and Armadillo is thirsty. But he doesn't have enough money for a glass of lemonade at Rabbit's stand. Somehow he will have to work for the lemonade. First he dances, but that isn't good enough. He juggles, but hits Rabbit on the head with a lemon. Just when it seems he may never get any lemonade, Armadillo comes up with an idea that is just right.

This group of three stories about Armadillo and his friends Turtle and Rabbit will amuse and delight beginning readers.

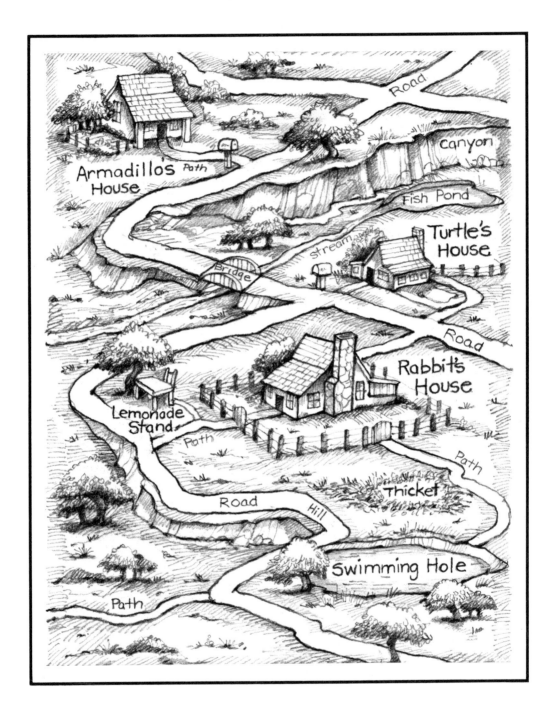

A LET ME READ BOOK

Ida Luttrell

NOT LIKE THAT, ARMADILLO

ILLUSTRATED BY

Janet Stevens

HARCOURT BRACE JOVANOVICH, PUBLISHERS
NEW YORK AND LONDON

TO MY MOTHER

Helen Harbison

AND FOUR OF HER GRANDCHILDREN

Bob, Anne, Billy, and Richard

Printed in the United States of America

LIBRARY OF CONGRESS CATALOGING IN PUBLICATION DATA
Luttrell, Ida.   Not like that, Armadillo   (A Let me read book)
Contents: Lemonade — Armadillo's book — The lucky penny.
[1. Animals—Fiction] I. Stevens, Janet, ill.   II. Title. III. Series.
PZ7.L97953No   [E]   81-20107
ISBN 0-15-257584-7   ISBN 0-15-257585-5 (pbk.)   AACR2
B   C   D   E   FIRST EDITION   B   C   D   E (PBK.)

CONTENTS

NOT LIKE THAT, ARMADILLO

LEMONADE

Armadillo sat in the shade of a cactus.
It was hot, very hot. He saw his friend Turtle
walking down the road.

"Turtle," he cried, "where are you going?"

"To Rabbit's lemonade stand," Turtle said.
"I am thirsty."

"Wait for me," Armadillo said. "I will come
with you. It is a good day for lemonade."

"Yes," Turtle said, "it is a lemonade kind of
day."

So they walked and walked, down the road,
around the bend, to the crooked old tree,
where Rabbit had his lemonade stand.

Rabbit sat behind the stand and waited for
customers. There were some glasses, a
pitcher of lemonade, and a basket of lemons
on the stand. Next to it was a sign that said,
"Lemonade 5¢. Refills 2¢."

"Hello, friends," Rabbit said. "What can I
do for you today?"

"Hello, Rabbit," said Armadillo.

"Hi, Rabbit," said Turtle. "I would like a
glass of lemonade."

"Very good," said Rabbit. "And how about you, Armadillo?"

"I will have one refill," Armadillo said. And he put two cents on the stand.

Rabbit laughed. "You can't have a refill," he said. "First you have to drink one glass of lemonade. Then you can have a refill."

"But I do not want the first glass of lemonade," Armadillo said. "Your sign says, 'Lemonade 5¢. Refills 2¢.' All I have is two cents. I just want the refill."

"Refill means fill it again. I can't fill it again," said Rabbit, "unless it was full before. I am sorry, but you can't have a refill. Come back when you have five cents. Then you can have some lemonade."

"Can I work for it?" asked Armadillo.

"There is nothing to do," Rabbit said. "I have washed the glasses. I have made the lemonade. And Turtle is the only customer I have had today."

Turtle smiled. He felt important.

"I know what,"
Armadillo said.

"I will do a dance
for you."

He stood on his toes and whirled around.
He kicked his legs and jumped in the air. He
sailed past Turtle and fell flat at Rabbit's feet.

Rabbit looked at Armadillo. He shook his
head. "That was not worth a cent," he said.
"You will have to do better than that."

"Armadillo, I will give you some of my lemonade," Turtle said.

"No, thank you, Turtle. You are thirsty, and that is your lemonade. You drink it. I will get my own."

Armadillo turned to Rabbit. "Rabbit, I have thought of something," he said.

"What?" asked Rabbit.

"I will juggle for you," Armadillo said.

"What are you going to juggle?" asked Turtle.

"Yes, what?" asked Rabbit.

Armadillo looked all around. "I am going to juggle lemons!" he said.

Before Rabbit could say no, Armadillo took
three lemons from the basket. He threw them
up all at once. They went flying everywhere.

One went up in a tree and fell through an
old bird's nest. One rolled under the table.

The last one hit Rabbit on the head.

"Armadillo," said Rabbit in a cross voice, "forget juggling."

Rabbit picked up the lemons and put them in the basket.

"We had better leave," said Turtle.

"Not yet," said Armadillo. "I have thought of something else. Rabbit," he said, "I bet you don't know something."

"What?" asked Rabbit.

"Where lemonade comes from," said Armadillo.

"Yes I do," Rabbit said. "I just made some."

"No, no," Armadillo said. "I mean the first lemonade—where it came from long ago."

"Where *did* it come from?" asked Rabbit.

"If I tell you the story," Armadillo asked, "will you give me a refill for two cents?"

"It had better be a good story," said Rabbit.

So Armadillo began.

"Long ago I had a cousin who lived in the land of milk and honey. Every day he had milk and honey for breakfast, lunch, and dinner. Cousin was sick of milk and honey. The milk was not tasty, and the honey was full of dead bees.

"One day he saw a lemon hanging from a tree. He took a bite of it. 'Wow!' he said. 'That is too sour! But I like the flavor. I will mix the juice with water. Then it will not be too sour.' So he did. But it was still too sour.

"That night he could not get lemons out of
his mind. When he went to sleep, he dreamed
of lemon-juice lakes and mountains of snow-
white sugar.

"Cousin woke up and jumped out of bed. 'Of course,' he cried, 'sugar is the answer. Sugar will sweeten the lemon juice.' So he mixed lemon juice, sugar, and water.

"Then he tasted it. 'The perfect drink!' he cried. 'I shall call it lemonade.'

"And he *gave* it to all his friends. They all loved him and thought he was wonderful for *giving* them lemonade.

"*Now* do I get my lemonade?" asked
Armadillo.

Rabbit laughed. "I got the hint, Armadillo,"
he said. "I will *give* you a glass of lemonade,
and you will get a refill for two cents."

So Armadillo got his lemonade. He gave
the refill to Turtle, who was thirsty again.

ARMADILLO'S BOOK

"Look, Turtle, what came in the mail," Armadillo cried. He waved a book at Turtle, who was coming up the path.

"Let me see," said Turtle. "*Improve Your Body*," he read. "It looks like a good book."

"I am going for a swim. Swimming improves your body. Do you want to come with me?"

"No, Turtle, I will read my book. I will learn how to improve my body the right way."

"Suit yourself," said Turtle. "Swimming is fun. I will improve my body the fun way."

So Turtle headed for the swimming hole.

Armadillo sat beside the mailbox and read
his book. "Jogging is good for your body," he
read. "Then I will jog," said Armadillo, and
went to get his sneakers.

Armadillo jogged up the hill and down the road, by the swimming hole, and past Rabbit's lemonade stand. He jogged all morning. The sun rose higher. Armadillo was still jogging.

Turtle finished his swim and rested beside the swimming hole. Armadillo was still jogging.

Rabbit closed his lemonade stand for the day and went home. Armadillo was still jogging.

The sun went down and the moon came up.
Armadillo jogged home and went to bed.

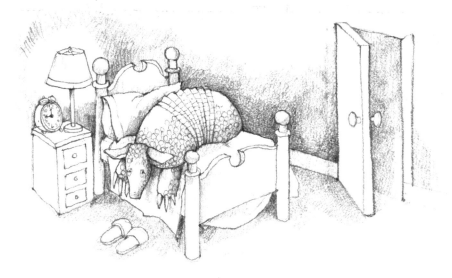

The next morning Turtle was at his door.

"Good morning, Armadillo," he said, "are you going to jog this morning?"

"No," said Armadillo, "my feet hurt. My legs don't want to move. I will try something else."

He took out his book.

"What is next?" asked Turtle.

Armadillo read, "Bananas are good for your skin."

"Good," said Armadillo, "I have lots of bananas."

Armadillo peeled a banana and rubbed it on his legs, on his face, and on the back of his neck.

"Armadillo, I think you were supposed to eat the banana," said Turtle.

"No," said Armadillo, and he showed the page to Turtle. "It says right here, 'Bananas are good for your skin.'"

The banana on Armadillo's skin began to turn brown.

"Let's get some fresh air," Turtle said. "We can go for a walk."

Armadillo remembered his feet. "I would rather sit in the sun," he said.

So they sat in the sun outside Armadillo's
door. A fly came and buzzed around
Armadillo's face. Then another fly came and
another and another. Soon there were many
flies buzzing around Armadillo.

Turtle stood up. "I think I will go now."

"Don't go, Turtle. I will see what is next."
Armadillo opened his book.

"Singing helps," he read. "I like to sing,"
said Armadillo.

He pointed his nose to the sky and began
to sing.

"Excuse me," said Turtle, "but . . ."

Armadillo sang louder.

Turtle raised his voice. "Armadillo," he said, "I hate to tell you, but . . ."

Armadillo sang louder, and all the flies went home.

Rabbit came down the path. He covered
his ears.

Armadillo sang louder.

Turtle shouted, "That singing doesn't help!"

But Armadillo did not hear him, so Turtle
left. Armadillo sang all day and half the night.

The next morning Turtle knocked on
Armadillo's door.

"Armadillo was very hoarse. "Come in," he
whispered. "Turtle, do you want to go for a
swim?"

"Yes," Turtle answered, "but where is your book?"

"Where it helps my body best," said Armadillo. And he pointed to his bed. Turtle saw the book under Armadillo's pillow.

"My pillow," said Armadillo, "has always seemed too flat."

THE LUCKY PENNY

Armadillo was walking down the road. The road was dry and full of cracks. Armadillo was taking short, funny steps. His friend Turtle saw him.

"What are you doing, Armadillo?"

"Stepping on cracks," said Armadillo. "Step on a crack and save your mother's back."

"No, no, Armadillo," Turtle said. "It is, 'Step on a crack and break your mother's back.'"

"But I always step on cracks," said Armadillo, "and my mother's back is not broken."

Turtle walked along with Armadillo. Armadillo stepped on another crack. He saw something shining in the road, and he picked it up.

"Aha," he said, "I found a penny. 'Find a penny and pick it up, and all the day you will have good luck.' "

"Oh, no, Armadillo," Turtle said. "It goes like this, 'Find a pin and pick it up and all the day you will have good luck.' "

"I would rather have a penny," Armadillo said. "I can wish on a penny."

"Only if you throw it in a wishing well," said Turtle. "There is no wishing well here."

"I can still wish on it," Armadillo insisted.

"But the wish won't come true," said Turtle. "You must throw the penny in something."

Turtle thought a minute. "I know," he said, "you can throw it in the swimming hole."

"That is a good idea," said Armadillo. So they hurried to the swimming hole.

Rabbit was already there.

"Look, Rabbit," Armadillo said, "I found a penny. I will make a wish on it."

"It is silly to wish on pennies," said Rabbit. "Pennies are for saving."

Armadillo did not listen.

"Now I will make my wish," said Armadillo.
He went to the edge of the swimming hole
and closed his eyes tight. In a loud voice he
said, "I wish for a watermelon."

"Not like *that*," Turtle cried. "If someone

hears your wish, it will not come true."

Turtle was too late. The penny hit the water and so did Armadillo.

"What is he doing?" asked Turtle.

Rabbit rolled his eyes and sighed. "Who knows?" he said. "That is just like him."

Turtle and Rabbit watched the water and
waited for Armadillo. But Armadillo did not
come back.

Turtle looked on one side of the swimming
hole. Rabbit ran to the other side and looked.
But Armadillo was not there.

Turtle began to cry. "I am worried," he
said. "It is all my fault. I told Armadillo to
throw the penny in the swimming hole."

"Nonsense," said Rabbit, "you did not tell
him to jump in too. I will count to three. If he
is not out by then, we will go in after him."

"One, two, three," Rabbit counted. Still no Armadillo. So Rabbit and Turtle jumped in the swimming hole.

Armadillo came up sputtering and splashing.
He was covered with mud and out of breath.

"There he is!" cried Turtle. He and Rabbit
climbed out of the swimming hole.

Rabbit shook the water out of his ears. "What were you doing?" he asked Armadillo.

"Looking for my penny," said Armadillo. "I wanted to make more wishes, but now my penny is gone."

"What did you expect?" asked Rabbit. "You threw it away, and just look at us. Now we are all wet."

"Your penny may be gone, Armadillo," said Turtle, "but I am glad you are here."

"And I did make one wish," said Armadillo, "so I will get a watermelon."

"Don't count on it," said Rabbit.

Turtle reminded Armadillo, "You did make that wish out loud."

"No matter," said Armadillo, "pennies are lucky and wishes come true."

"We will have to go to my house and dry
off," grumbled Rabbit. So they started down
the path to his house.

They walked through a thicket where
someone had been on a picnic. Armadillo saw
something red and green on the ground.

"Look," Armadillo cried, "my wish has come true!"

"That is nothing but a watermelon rind," said Rabbit. "You wished for a watermelon."

"But look at all the seeds," said Armadillo. "I will plant a garden and grow lots of watermelons."

Turtle grinned.

"I will help you," he said. "Because I love watermelon."

ABOUT THE AUTHOR

Ida Luttrell was born and raised in Texas. After graduating from the University of Texas with a degree in bacteriology, she worked for a number of years at the Texas Children's Hospital. She now lives in Houston with her husband, William, and is the mother of four children.

ABOUT THE ARTIST

Janet Stevens, who has always loved drawing animals, has illustrated a number of books for children, including *Animal Fair* and *The Princess and the Pea.* Ms. Stevens is a graduate of the University of Colorado and now lives in a small town outside Boulder with her husband, Ted, their cats, and their daughter, Lindsey.